A Dream for Addie

by Gail Rock

Illustrated by Charles C. Gehm

A YEARLING BOOK

Published by
Dell Publishing Co., Inc.
1 Dag Hammarskjold Plaza
New York, New York 10017

For Lisa Lucas, who is sometimes more like me than I am.

Yearling ® TM 913705, Dell Publishing Co., Inc.

ISBN: 0-440-42151-9

Reprinted by arrangement with Alfred A. Knopf, Inc.

Printed in the United States of America

April 1986

10 9 8 7 6 5 4 3 2

CW

With acknowledgments to Alan Shayne, Paul Bogart and Pat Ross for their creative friendship.

A Dream for Addie

Prologue

I'M AN ARTIST NOW, and I live and work in the city. With all the cement and noise and cars, the coming of spring seems to pass almost unnoticed. When I was growing up in Nebraska in the 1940s, the subtle signs of spring were one of the great pleasures of my life. It was always a contest at our house to see who could spot the first robin on the lawn, and we all watched eagerly for the morning when Grandma's daffodils would burst into bloom outside the kitchen door. To me, Easter always meant sewing a new Sunday dress and dyeing eggs until my fingers were stained like a rainbow. But the Easter I remember best was in 1948 when I was twelve years old.

Chapter One

SINCE IT WAS EASTER VACATION TIME and I didn't have to go to school that morning, I didn't really have any reason to get up. But I got up anyway, because around our house if you didn't get up, there had to be some reason. Only sick or dying or slothful people stayed in bed late. Since neither Dad nor Grandma nor I would even think of committing the sin of sloth, staying in bed late at our house meant you were probably at death's door. Then you had to eat milk toast and get mentholatum up your nose and iodine down your throat and a thermometer under your tongue until you realized that getting up early was a terrific idea after all. That's why I always got up early even when I didn't have to.

Besides, I liked eating breakfast when Dad and Grandma were at the table too. My mother had died more than eleven years ago, just after I was born, and Grandma had come to live with Dad and me then. Grandma was in her seventies and short and wrinkled. Anybody who didn't know better might have thought to look at her that she was a frail old lady. Dad and I knew better. Grandma was a powerful, energetic little bundle. She was the first one up in the morning and the last one to bed at night, and she outworked a lot of my friends' mothers who were half her age. She had such strong hands she could put the lid on a pickle jar too tight for even my father to remove it.

Grandma didn't just keep house either. She had the biggest and best vegetable garden in the neighborhood and more flowers and fruit trees than anybody in town. She did more sewing and baking and canning than anyone else and still found time to sit and read for an hour or two every day. Her favorite books were her Bible and her dictionary, and she kept them right by her rocking chair in the living room so she could look things up at any time. She loved helping me with my vocabulary and spelling lessons, and we would always give each other the word tests in the *Reader's Digest* when the new issue arrived.

Grandma was reading at the table that morning and so was Dad, so there wasn't much conversation. It was Thursday, the day the little town paper, the *Clear River Clarion* came out, and they were both busy catching up on the local news. Actually there was never anything in the *Clarion* that everybody in town hadn't already known for days, but somehow seeing it down in black and white made it seem more important.

While they read, I silently finished my oatmeal with raisins and apples cut up in it. Then I got some eggs out of the refrigerator. Using one of Grandma's hatpins, I poked holes in both ends of the eggshells and blew the raw egg out into a bowl. I had been doing this for weeks to get eggshells to decorate for Easter, and so we had been having a lot of scrambled eggs lately.

I never believed in doing one thing at a time because it seemed wasteful, so while I was huffing and puffing into the eggshells, I decided to read the back of Dad's section of the paper. It wasn't easy, with my glasses sliding down my nose and my pigtails swinging precariously close to the bowl of raw egg. I pushed the bowl of egg closer to Dad and gave a particularly hard puff. The egg slurped noisily out into the bowl as I leaned in closer to his paper. He suddenly whipped the paper up over his head and looked right into my face, which by that time was practically over his bowl of oatmeal.

"Will you get your face out of my lap, Addie?" he said, irritated. Then he looked down at the bowl of raw egg. "And don't do that mess at the table . . . it's disgusting."

"Sorry," I mumbled. I seemed to have a talent for irritating Dad. I didn't intend to, but it usually worked out that way. I knew we liked each other, but he wasn't very good at showing it, and some of that seemed to rub off on me when he and I were together. Most of the time it was a friendly battle, though.

Dad was tall and slender, and his dark hair was just beginning to gray at the temples. He had a plain Midwestern face that always reminded me of those tight-lipped cowboys in the movies. Though he was easily annoyed by me, we had some good times together, and I was slowly learning how to hold my own with him.

I leaned in close to his paper again, and he looked over at me.

"I don't know what's so important in this rag of a paper that you can't wait till I'm finished," he said.

"I wanna see if there's anything in it about our Easter Style Show contest."

"What's that?" he asked.

"Oh, Dad! I told you about it a million times! All the

sixth grade girls are designing original fashion creations for the 4-H Club."

"Fashion creations!" he said, sounding disgusted. "I thought you were making dresses."

"Oh, Dad! You know what I mean! And we're having a contest to see who does the best one. We're going to model them at the Women's Club luncheon next week, and they'll pick the winner."

"Oh, well," he said sarcastically. "Big news like that wouldn't be in the town paper . . . that's probably on the front page of the *Omaha World Herald!*"

"Very funny!" I said, looking disgusted. The *Omaha World Herald* was Nebraska's biggest newspaper, and we read it every day, even though it never seemed to report anything about the people in Clear River.

"You going to school looking like that?" Dad asked, eyeing my old jeans.

I didn't care much for dressing up, but I was not allowed to wear jeans to school. "Dad!" I said. "It's Easter vacation! I don't have to go to school for two whole weeks!"

"Well, I'll be!" Grandma interrupted from behind her paper.

"What?" I asked.

"The paper says Constance Gunderson is back here from New York," said Grandma. "Says she attended her mother's funeral in Omaha and is out here in Clear River to sell the family home."

"Huh!" snorted Dad. "She'll never unload that white elephant. Must have twenty rooms in the joint. Nobody could afford to heat it in the winter."

I figured I knew everybody in Clear River, but this was all new to me. "Is that the big house on Elm Street, the empty one? Who's Constance Gunderson? What does she do in New York?" I asked.

"What are you, the district attorney?" said Dad.

"Well, who is she?" I asked impatiently.

"She's Constance Payne, the actress," said Grandma. "That's her stage name. I guess she didn't like Gunderson for acting."

"I never saw her in any movies, did I?" I asked.

"She's never been in any," said Dad.

"She's on the stage," Grandma said. "She does those Broadway things."

"You mean real, live theater stuff?" I asked, fascinated.

"Yeah," said Dad, sounding unimpressed. "Probably Shakespeare and all that highbrow stuff. Don't know why anybody would want to sit through that after a hard day's work."

I was about to go on with my cross-examination when my best friend Carla Mae knocked on the door. Carla Mae lived next door, and she was my age. She had a knack of showing up at our house just at mealtime. This amused my grandmother, who loved to feed everybody, but annoyed my father, who thought it was a conspiracy to cost him more money—the thing he worried about most. The truth was that Carla Mae just liked to eat. She would have a meal at home and then drop over and have another one with us. She was beginning to look a bit on the chubby side.

I opened the door and yanked her inside in a hurry, so I wouldn't miss any of the talk about Constance Payne.

"Kid! Wait'll you hear what I just heard!" I hissed at her.

"What?"

"Constance Payne, the Broadway actress, is coming to Clear River!"

"Who?" she asked, looking confused.

"Already had breakfast, Carla Mae?" Grandma interrupted.

"Yeah, but I could stand some oatmeal, I guess."

"I thought so," Grandma smiled. Dad gave an irritated little grunt from behind his paper.

I shoved Carla Mae into a chair, and Grandma plopped a bowl of oatmeal down in front of her.

"Who's Constance Payne?" Carla Mae asked, "I never heard of her."

"That's what I'm trying to find out!" I said impatiently, and continued with my barrage of questions to Dad and Grandma.

We learned that the Gundersons had been one of the few wealthy families in Clear River and that they hadn't socialized much with other folks in town. Constance was only a couple of years younger than Dad, and they had attended high school together. Then she had gone East to an exclusive women's college and to England to study drama and had gone on the stage in New York.

She was beginning to sound very glamorous to me. Grandma said that Constance had come back to Clear River only once before, when her father had died some years ago. After that her mother had lived on alone in the old family house, a huge Victorian monstrosity that was on the edge of town. Then Mrs. Gunderson had taken ill and was moved to an Omaha nursing home where she had died a week ago. There had been no notice of her Omaha funeral in the paper, so nobody from

Clear River had attended. Now it seemed that Constance Payne was in our town between engagements and would be selling the house, never to return.

"What was she like?" I asked Dad.

"Oh, she was always puttin' on airs," he said, sounding uninterested.

"Do you think she has her name in lights? Is she really a big star?" I asked.

"I guess so," said Grandma. "Her folks always said she was doin' real good."

"What does she look like, Dad? Have you seen her since she became a star?"

"Oh, she's pretty, I guess. Dark-haired. When she came back for her father's funeral, she didn't stay around long enough to talk to anybody."

Dad wasn't much on telling details, and at a time like this it was infuriating.

"Well did you ever go out with her?"

"Ha!" he snorted. "Are you kidding? She was too fancy for me!"

"Wow!" said Carla Mae, now finally caught up in the excitement. "I wish we could go to New York and see her!"

"Listen," I said. "We can go see her right here!"

"I mean in a play," she said.

"Yeah, but at least we could get her autograph. We'll just go over there and . . ."

"No!" said Dad. "I don't want you going over there and pestering her."

"Oh, James," said Grandma, giving Carla Mae and me a sympathetic look. "I can't see it would hurt anything."

Grandma was always more understanding of our brainstorms and projects than Dad was.

"I don't want her hanging around some . . . actress!" He said it as though it were a dirty word.

"Gosh, Dad. All we want is her autograph. We're not going to move in with her!"

"Well, you just stay away from there. Her folks were nothing but rich trash."

That bit of news intrigued Carla Mae and me, but we didn't have a chance to follow it up.

"Now, James," said Grandma. She didn't like to hear unkind gossip.

"Well, Mother, neither one of them ever did a day's work in their lives," said Dad.

"You can't blame her for the way her folks behaved," said Grandma. "She was always a nice girl in school. You used to say so yourself."

"Oh, I hardly knew her," Dad grumbled, and he got up to get his lunch pail.

Carla Mae and I grabbed the paper Grandma had been reading and leaned our heads together over the table to read the article about Constance Payne.

"When does she get here?" Carla Mae whispered.

"According to this, she's here now!" I hissed back. We gave each other one of our looks that said we were darn well going to see Constance Payne the actress if we had to go all the way to New York City and buy a ticket to Shakespeare.

Carla Mae was having a slumber party at her house that night so she and I and Gloria Cott and Tanya Smithers (my worst friend in the sixth grade) could work on our Easter Style Show dresses. I didn't really want to participate because I hated sewing, but it was the big yearly project of our 4-H Club, so I had to do it. The Women's Club cooperated by letting us present our creations at their luncheon and then awarded a prize for the best dress.

As long as I had no choice about being in the show, I was determined to do something creative. I had selected a simple dress pattern and was adding my own artistic details to it. The other three girls laid their dress patterns out on the floor so they could work as we talked, but I was still sketching in some of the artistic details I was adding, and I was going to keep it a secret until the day of the show.

We cracked our gum loudly as we worked because Tanya had recently revealed that she hated to hear people crack gum, and since then we had been doing it a lot.

Carla Mae had a lot of brothers and sisters—three of each in fact—so we all took our own blankets and pillows along and planned to sleep on the floor in her room. Actually, we didn't plan to sleep at all, as that was the whole point of slumber parties. Another point was eating, and we always cooked our favorite stuff. Our usual combination was fudge and french fried potatoes. It made my dad sick just to hear the two things mentioned in the same sentence, but we loved it.

There was always an argument over whether to put walnuts in the fudge. I hated them because I thought fudge should be enjoyed in its pure state. Tanya and Carla Mae liked the crunch of walnuts between their teeth, and Gloria, who never liked to argue about anything, just didn't care. So we always made one fourth of the pan pure fudge, and that was for me. We were eating it with our french fried potatoes while we talked about the style show.

Tanya's mother was about the only woman in town la-de-da enough to read *Vogue* and *Bazaar*, and Tanya had brought along some old copies for us to use as inspiration. Tanya was studying them carefully and writing something down.

"What are you writing?" asked Gloria.

"I'm copying some of my style show narration out of *Vogue*," said Tanya.

We all groaned.

"How come?" asked Carla Mae.

"I want to make sure it fits in with our theme, High Society Steps Out," Tanya said.

We had worked for weeks to find just the right, sophisticated theme idea.

"Ugh!" said Gloria. "I hate the whole thing. It's so embarrassing to walk up and down in front of all those people!"

I felt about the same way, but I didn't let on. I always hated to admit I was afraid of anything.

I leaned back on the bed with my sketch pad and put a few more touches on my design. "Oh, I don't know if I'm ever going to get the details right on this dress!" I said, trying to build up the suspense for the others.

"Let's see it," Carla Mae said, and reached for my pad.

"No!" I said. "I told you it's a secret design until the show!"

"OK," she said, annoyed. "Who cares?"

The three of them studiously ignored me, pretending to be interested in Tanya's copy of *Vogue*.

"Oh, this is so complicated!" I sighed, trying to tantalize them. "It really is the most elaborate thing I've ever designed!"

Tanya turned and gave me a dirty look. "For somebody who hates to sew, you're sure making a big deal out of this," she said.

"Well, I wouldn't even be in the dumb style show if I didn't have to," I said. "But if I have to do it, I'm going to be creative, and believe me, this is creee-ative!"

"Oh, come on, let's see what you're doing," said Gloria. "You've seen all of ours." She reached toward me.

"No!" I said, pulling the sketch pad away.

Suddenly Carla Mae lunged across the bed at me. "Lemme see it, Mills!" she shouted, and dived for the sketch pad.

"No! You rat!" I screamed, and scrambled to get away.

Then Tanya and Gloria jumped across the bed too, and we were in a wild free-for-all. I rolled into a ball, clutching the pad to my stomach, and they pinched, tickled and clobbered me with pillows, trying to get it away. I screamed as loud as I could, which was ear-splitting.

"Shhhh!" said Carla Mae quickly, and pulled off the other two. "You'll wake up my folks, and they'll kill me!"

"OK," I said. "Get away from me then. Truce!"

They backed off, giving up. I had kept my secret design from them.

"Immature!" I snarled at them, as I readjusted my glasses and settled myself on the bed again.

"It better be some fancy dress when we see it," said Gloria.

I retrieved my gum from the bedpost, where I had put it when I was eating my fudge and french fries, and Tanya glared at me and turned up her nose. Tanya imagined herself to have the most refined manners of the four of us. I put my sketch pad safely away and started leafing idly through *Vogue*.

We wanted to have someone special in town present the awards for the best designs at the style show, and we discussed all the possible town celebrities. There was Miss Thompson, our favorite teacher, but she had presented the awards the year before. There was Mrs. Clauson, the banker's wife, who was the richest woman in town, but we counted her out because she was fat and not very stylish herself. Of course, Tanya wanted her mother to be the presenter, but we all ruled that out in a hurry, with much cracking of gum.

"Think of someone!" Carla Mae said, and we were silent for a few moments.

"These fashion magazines are so stupid!" I said, as I continued looking through them. "I wouldn't be caught dead at a dogfight in these clothes!"

Just then, Tanya pulled out a bottle of dark red nail polish and a big wad of cotton from her overnight bag.

"Gad!" said Carla Mae. "Where did you get that."

"I borrowed it from my mother," Tanya said haughtily.

None of us were allowed to use nail polish or any other make up until we were in high school, and we stared at it enviously.

"Does your mother let you wear nail polish now?" Gloria asked.

"Only at night," said Tanya. "I have to take it off before I go out in the morning."

We all groaned.

"That's ridiculous!" I said.

"Well," said Tanya smugly. "When we're old enough to wear nail polish, I'm going to know how to do it, and you're not."

She proceeded to put big wads of cotton between her toes to hold them apart and then started painting her toenails as we all watched in fascination. I didn't want to give her the satisfaction of looking too interested, so I went back to my magazine.

" 'What to Wear to a Broadway Opening Night' " I read from one of the articles.

"We've got to think of somebody to present the awards!" Carla Mae said impatiently.

Suddenly I got one of my brilliant brainstorms.

"Constance Payne!" I shouted at them.

"Addie!" said Carla Mae. "We were going to keep that a secret!"

"Oh, I know!" I said. "But I just got this brainstorm! She's the perfect person to present the awards!"

"What secret?" demanded Tanya. "Constance who?"

Carla Mae and I excitedly told Tanya and Gloria the story of Constance Gunderson Payne, interrupting each other with all the glamorous details and embroidering a bit on what we already knew. I announced that we had planned to visit her anyway to ask for an autograph. Tanya glared at me. It was just the kind of dramatic announcement she would have loved to make herself.

"And you weren't going to tell us?" Tanya said, furious.

"We would've told you later," I said.

"Thanks a lot!" she said huffily.

"What does she look like?" asked Gloria.

"I don't know exactly," I said. "But she has to be fabulous!"

"How do you know?" Gloria asked.

"Leading ladies have to be glamorous," Carla Mae said.

"OK, it's settled," I said. "When I get her autograph, I'll ask her to be our celebrity guest."

"Who elected you?" Tanya asked. "We'll all go."

"Well," I said, in my best snob-lady accent, "I'm sure she doesn't want a lot of strange people descending on her house unannounced. Perhaps I should go alone."

"Listen, kiddo," said Carla Mae, annoyed. "It was my idea, too, to get her autograph!"

"Yeah," said Tanya. "It's a free country. Anybody can go up to her house if they want."

"Oh, all right," I said. "But I'll do the asking when it comes to the moment of truth."

Tanya was about to give me a smart answer when she looked down at her feet. "Oh, no!" she shrieked. "All my toes are stuck to the cotton!" We all hooted and cracked our gum right in her ears.

Chapter Two

THE NEXT DAY, contrary to my father's instructions to stay away, the four of us set off to see Constance Payne. Clear River was so small, we only had to walk about five blocks to get to the Gunderson house. We went around 3 P.M., because, as I had pointed out to everyone, "Actresses always sleep late."

I had picked some of the daffodils that were just beginning to bloom around the back corner of our little house, and took them along for Miss Payne. We dressed in our best clothes, and all carried our autograph books. On the way over, there was a lot of serious discussion about who had the best autograph collection. My best autograph was Roy Rogers, who had signed my book at a parade in Omaha. Tanya was bragging about her autograph from Margaret Truman, but I told her it didn't count because she got it through the mail, and autographs weren't for real unless you got them from the actual person in the flesh. Tanya said snippily that she would rather have Margaret Truman in the mail than Roy Rogers in the flesh, and I told her that was a sign of her rotten taste.

There was also a lot of discussion about what Constance Payne might look like. Nobody in Clear River had seen her for years, and other than my father saying that she was pretty and dark-haired, we didn't know what to expect. Gloria speculated that she might have bleached her hair and look like our favorite movie star, Betty Grable, but I pooh-poohed that idea because I knew stage acting was supposed to be high-class and not pin-up stuff like the movies.

Tanya was still a bit miffed because Carla Mae and I had come up with this adventure, and she walked ahead a few steps with me to tell me something confidentially.

"My father said that when they were in school Constance Payne was always flirting with him, but he never went out with her because she wasn't his type." She looked at me smugly.

I knew she had made it up, and I wasn't about to let her get away with it.

"Well," I said. "My father knew her very well. I think she was mad for him. They dated a lot." I plunged on recklessly, "I bet she can't wait to see him again. She'll want to come over for dinner, I suppose."

"For dinner?" she asked, scornfully. "At your house?"

"Yes," I said, putting on my la-de-da accent, "I suppose I really should invite her for some Saturday evening."

Tanya was about to make a rude reply when the others walked up beside us. We were there.

I was feeling a bit nervous as we approached the big old house. No one had lived in it since we could remember, and we had always jokingly referred to it as the haunted mansion. Of course, we didn't take that seriously, but I wondered just what kind of welcome we would get from Constance Payne. She might not want a bunch of kids hanging around.

We trooped up on the porch, and I knocked on the door a

few times. There was no answer, and after a few moments, I knocked again, louder. The house was so big, we wondered if she would ever hear it.

"Oh, come on, let's go!" said Tanya. "She's not even here."

"Relax!" I answered.

"Well, she's not going to say yes to the style show anyway," Tanya said. "It's stupid to ask her."

I had a feeling Tanya would be secretly pleased if Constance said no. We waited nervously. Finally we heard footsteps approaching the door, and we all self-consciously tugged at our socks and dresses and tried to make ourselves presentable.

The door opened, and there stood Constance Payne. We were all so overwhelmed by her appearance that for a moment we said nothing. We just stood and stared at her.

I thought she was the most dramatic, exotic person I had ever seen. She looked a bit sleepy and disheveled, with her dark hair tousled about her face, but she was very beautiful. She was wearing an elegant black kimono splashed with big red flowers, and she wore dark red nail polish and strange, embroidered slippers.

She was staring back at us with a slightly irritated expression. I thought I had better say something before she closed the door in our faces.

"Constance Payne?" I asked stupidly. As though it could be anyone else!

"Yes?" she said in a low, rich voice, sounding impatient.

"I'm Addie Mills . . . I mean Adelaide." I quickly thrust the daffodils at her. "These are for you. To welcome you to Clear River. I mean, to welcome you back."

She took the flowers. "Well, thank you, Adelaide," she said, and moved back as though she were going to close the door.

"You can call me Addie," I said quickly, trying desperately to make conversation. Carla Mae gave out a big "ah-hem" behind me, and I suddenly remembered to introduce the other three girls.

Then Tanya blurted out, "Could we have your autograph?" I elbowed her, furious at her bad manners for asking so soon.

Constance tried to make some excuse about not having time or doing it some other day, but the three of them persisted, and she finally agreed. Then we discovered that none of us had a pen, and Tanya had the nerve to ask if we could borrow one.

"I must have a pen inside somewhere," Constance said. "Excuse me." She turned to go, leaving the door ajar. That was all the invitation we needed, and we rushed in behind her and followed her through the big dark hall and into the parlor on the right. When she realized we were behind her, she stopped suddenly and spun around. I thought she was going to throw us out, and we all froze in our tracks. She looked at us for a moment and then gave a sigh and went on into the room and walked over to a big trunk. We followed, taking in the surroundings as we went. It was a dark old room, full of red plush furniture and ornate lamps. Some of the furniture was covered with sheets, and a big carpet was rolled up against one wall. The old trunk was obviously one that had belonged to Constance. It was plastered with travel stickers from cities in Europe and full of little drawers and compartments.

There was a pair of sunglasses on top of the trunk, and she picked them up and put them on. I wondered why. I had never

seen anyone wear sunglasses indoors, and I imagined from that moment on that all actresses did.

Tanya, Gloria and Carla Mae gathered around the trunk as Constance searched for a pen, but I didn't want to appear over-anxious, so I became interested in some old posters leaning against a table. They announced her appearances in several plays in cities back East. I had never heard of some of the towns, but the plays sounded glamorous. She must have sent the posters home to her family earlier in her career.

"I'm afraid the house is in a bit of a mess," she was saying. "I'm sorting through things, trying to get it all settled before I go back to New York."

"I bet you travel a lot," I said, still looking at the posters. "Like on tours and all that."

"Well, yes, sometimes I work outside of New York," she said, sounding distracted. "Here's a pen."

Tanya, Gloria and Carla Mae all shoved their autograph books at her, but I hung back, trying to be polite. When she finished with the others, Constance turned to me and held out her hand for my book.

"And you're Adelaide?" she said, starting to write.

"Make it to 'Addie.' I hate 'Adelaide,'" I said, making a face about my awful name.

"I always hated my last name," she said, looking at me for a moment. "'Gunderson' didn't seem right for the theater, so I changed it."

"That's what I'm going to do!" I said. "I don't want to sign my paintings 'Adelaide.' It'll look stupid."

She looked up from my book. "Are you an artist?"

"Well, I'm gonna be one . . . as soon as I can go to Paris and New York and study and stuff."

"New York?" she asked, seeming surprised.

"Oh, yeah! I'm going the day I get out of college. I can't wait! I've got a scrapbook about New York, and a map and everything."

Tanya made a face. "Oh, she's always talking about having her paintings in the Museum of Metropolitan Art!"

"It's the Metropolitan Museum of Art, dodo!" I snapped back at her. I knew she couldn't stand it that Constance and I were having this whole sophisticated conversation. I turned to Constance. "I hope I'll be a success like you. Then there'll be two famous people from Clear River."

She looked away from me when I said that, and put the pen back in a drawer of the trunk. Then she started for the door as though to usher us out. We followed on her heels, all talking at once, asking questions about her life in New York. I couldn't take my eyes off her. I had never been that close to anyone so glamorous. She tried to be polite, but I could tell she didn't really want to answer our questions and was anxious to get rid of us.

Tanya had the nerve to ask her if actresses make a lot of money, and Constance answered politely that leading ladies get paid very well. I informed Tanya that real actors don't act for the money, they do it for the love of the theater. It's a way of life! Constance seemed amused at that and made another move toward the door.

I thought I had better bring up the style show before it was too late.

"Are you going to be in town for a while?" I asked.

"I don't think so," she said.

"I suppose you have to start on a new play . . . rehearsals and all that?" said Carla Mae.

"What's your new play about?" asked Gloria.

Constance seemed to hesitate for a moment, and I interrupted. "Actresses don't discuss their roles before they rehearse. It's supposed to be a secret! Right?" I said to Constance.

She smiled at me. "Something like that, yes."

I thought I had made an impression on her by that knowledgeable remark about actresses, and it seemed a good time to launch into the invitation to the style show. We all bombarded her with requests, and I even assured her she wouldn't have to sit through the luncheon but could just come at the end of the show and hand out the awards. She listened patiently and then said, "I'm very flattered, but I really can't."

She moved to the door and opened it.

"I told you so," Tanya hissed. "You and your stupid ideas!"

I knew Constance had heard her. "Oh, clam up, will you?" I whispered angrily to Tanya.

"I'm sorry, but it's really impossible," Constance said, giving me an apologetic look.

"Oh, that's OK," I said, trying to save face. I moved to the door, ready to leave.

Suddenly Tanya grabbed my arm and said, in her phoniest "nice" voice, "Don't forget to invite Miss Payne to dinner Addie."

I could have killed her. She was putting me on the spot with my own fib, right in front of Constance.

"Oh, uh . . ." I stammered.

"Her father is your old friend, James Mills," Tanya said to Constance.

"James Mills?" Constance said, puzzled. "I don't think I remember . . ."

"Didn't you used to go out with him?" Tanya asked. "Addie said you did!"

I was flushed with embarrassment. "Well, it was a long time ago," I said to Constance. "Maybe you don't remember."

"Oh, James Mills!" Constance said suddenly. "I do remember him! He was a handsome devil. You tell him I said hello, won't you?" Somehow she had sensed what was happening and had helped me out. I couldn't believe it.

But Tanya was not about to let me off the hook. "Addie wanted you to come to dinner. She said you'd want to."

"Oh," I said, panicking again and trying to move toward the door. "I suppose you're too busy though."

"Maybe sometime soon," said Constance, trying to help me out again.

I began to go out, but Tanya grabbed my arm and pulled me back. "Her dad would just love to see you," she said to Constance. "It was his idea to invite you."

I saw a look of amazement on Carla Mae's face. She knew my dad better than that.

"You just let me know when," said Constance, trying to put an end to the conversation.

"Sure," I said, relieved and trying again to get out the door.

"She said it's for Saturday night!" Tanya said, with an evil smile on her face.

"Saturday?" Constance said, as though she wasn't really sure what we were talking about.

Suddenly I realized that I really wanted her to come to dinner, and I decided to plunge ahead.

"Uh, yeah," I said. "Saturday."

"Aren't you going to tell her what time?" asked Tanya, interrupting.

"We eat at six!" I said, and I rushed out the door before Constance could say no.

I heard her say, "Six?" in a puzzled voice, and then the others interrupted her with their good-byes before she could protest any further.

Tanya was the last one out the door, and she stopped and gave Constance a little curtsy and said in her gushiest voice, "Oh, thank you, Miss Payne, it was so fabulous! I've never met a real star before!"

As I looked back, I could see Constance standing in the gloomy old hallway, looking down at our bouquet of daffodils still in her hands.

I could have killed Tanya for what she had done, but on the other hand I was delighted that the dinner invitation had been made. My problem now was how to break the news to Grandma and Dad. Especially Dad.

By the time I got back to our house, Dad was home from work, and he and Grandma were out in back, working in the garden. It would soon be time for planting the earliest vegetables, and it was always part of my job to help get them in and keep them weeded through the summer. Today was the day for raking and cleaning out the garden plot and getting it ready.

Dad was still in his khaki work clothes and was busy laying out string to mark off the rows. Grandma was breaking up the clods of freshly spaded dirt with her hoe. She had on her usual gardening costume, a faded house dress and apron, old stockings with runs in them, moccasins and a huge straw hat. She looked part Indian, part Mexican and part little old lady.

Grandma was always careful to be presentable when she went out anywhere, but she thought it was a waste of good clothes to dress up at home. Sometimes I was embarrassed by the way she looked around the house, but most of my friends seemed not to notice her odd get-ups. They accepted her for what she was, and they all liked her lively personality and her interest in the things we did. She never minded having a houseful of us girls playing all-day Monopoly or planning a costume party or rehearsing one of our brilliant skits. She once told me it was because she didn't see or hear well enough to be disturbed by us, but I knew she was just kidding me and that she really liked having young people around because she enjoyed them.

I think Dad enjoyed my friends too, though he would never admit it. He would just pretend to be interested in his newspaper and would occasionally look up to ask how we could giggle so much without getting sick to our stomachs. I hoped he was in a good mood now, because I knew it was going to be a tricky situation.

"Hi!" I said, as I ran up to them in the garden. I was trying to sound casual, but I couldn't hide my excitement.

Grandma looked at my dress and knew something was going on.

"Where you been all dressed up?" she asked. I hated wearing anything fancier than jeans, and she knew it.

"We went to see Constance Payne and get her autograph." I held my book out to show her.

Dad turned around and looked at me. "I told you not to go over there," he said, annoyed.

"Oh, Dad, she was great," I said excitedly. "You should see her! She was wearing a fabulous Japanese kimono, black with great big red flowers, and these fantastic slippers with embroidery and sunglasses and bright red nail polish!"

"Sounds like the Dragon Lady to me," he said sarcastically.

"And the way she talks," I went on. "It's so elegant!"

"Most actors talk phony," he said, sounding unimpressed.

"Well, she studied in England," said Grandma. "I suppose she's got an accent."

"You should hear what she said about you," I said to Dad, teasing him.

"What?" he said, sounding curious.

"Oh, never mind!" I said, knowing he would be dying to find out. I thought it was a good way to distract him a bit before I told them about the dinner invitation.

"You can tell me," Grandma said, smiling and suspecting I was up to something.

"Well," I said, pausing dramatically, "I said, 'Do you remember James Mills?' And she said, 'Oh, he was a handsome devil!' "

Grandma and I both laughed, and Dad looked embarrassed. He didn't seem to know whether to believe it or not.

"How would she remember me?" he asked.

"She was positively exotic!" I went on. "And dramatic! And

nice, too. You really should see her. I asked her to present our style show awards, but she can't, she has to go back to New York . . . she's doing a new play on Broadway."

"I told you not to pester her!" Dad said. "It's not good manners to bother people that way."

"Oh, she didn't mind," I said. "Besides, I made up for it by inviting her to dinner." I winced, prepared for his reaction.

"You what?" he said.

"Oh, Addie!" said Grandma.

"Well, I had to! She said she wanted to see you again, Dad. I had to be polite. You just said to have good manners, didn't you?"

"You don't go inviting people to dinner without asking at home first!" he said angrily.

"Well, it's my home too!"

"Now, Addie, don't get sassy," said Grandma. "You really should have asked first."

"We can't have her here to dinner!" Dad said.

"Now, James," said Grandma. "It'll be all right."

"Can we have something special?" I asked Grandma, hoping to rush right on with the plans before Dad could stop it.

"We sure will," she replied. "I think it's a nice idea invitin' her. She's probably lonely in that big old house."

"Oh, Mother!" said Dad, exasperated. "She doesn't want to come to dinner over here!"

"The heck she doesn't!" I said. "She's coming Saturday night!"

The idea that it was all arranged for Saturday really seemed to set him off. "You had no business inviting her!" he shouted.

"You can just march right back over there and tell her you made a mistake. Tell her you forgot to ask your grandmother first."

"I can't do that." I said.

"Why not?" he asked.

"Well, she practically invited herself! And then, I told her you'd just *love* to see her again."

I thought he would explode at that. "I hardly know the fool woman!" he shouted.

Grandma was shushing him and trying not to smile. "Addie, that's fibbing! You mustn't do things like that."

"Well," I said, trying to hide my own smile, "Dad can always go over and tell her he doesn't want to see her, and that she can't come to dinner."

"Oh, brother!" he said, sounding defeated. "One of these days, I'm going to lock you up!"

Grandma and I smiled at each other and began to plan what to have for dinner on Saturday.

Chapter Three

I WAS AS NERVOUS AS A CAT all Saturday afternoon. I usually couldn't care less about clothes, but I tried on everything I owned about three times trying to look my best. I polished our old silver and shined the plates and glasses until my fingers ached. And I kept looking at the roast beef in the oven to see if it was going to be good enough for our special guest. I had made original place cards with artistic Easter motifs on them, and had picked some daffodils for a centerpiece. Grandma and I had moved the table from the kitchen to the living room in honor of Constance.

Dad looked absolutely disgusted by the whole thing, but when Grandma appeared in her best Sunday dress, he went and grudgingly put on a suit and tie.

When six o'clock arrived and Constance hadn't shown up, I began to get even more nervous. At six fifteen Dad looked at his watch and said she probably wasn't coming. He sounded pleased by the idea.

"She'll come!" I said. "I put a note under her door this afternoon to remind her. Besides, she's too high-class to just not show up!"

"High-class, my . . ." said Dad.

"James!" Grandma interrupted.

"Foot!" Dad finished.

There was a knock on the door, and I ran to answer it. Suddenly I hated our dumb, little four-room house. It was too threadbare, not good enough for Constance to see.

But there she was, looking quite beautiful. She had on a stylishly draped green dress, and her hair was curled and falling softly about her face. She carried a brown purse with beige gloves and wore brown pumps with open toes. I noticed a little chip on her fingernail polish that had been there the day we had met. She hadn't done her nails to come to dinner with us.

She seemed rather nervous and made an excuse about being late, saying she had tried to call but didn't realize we had no phone. I had a feeling she had wanted to call and say she wasn't coming at all, and for the first time in my life I was glad my thrifty father hadn't ever had a phone put in. Constance said she wouldn't be able to stay long because she was expecting an important call from New York. I put her bag and gloves down on a table near the door and introduced her to Dad and Grandma.

Dad seemed a bit uncomfortable having her there, and when she thanked him for inviting her to dinner, I thought he was going to blurt out that he had done no such thing. But he looked at me and covered it up nicely, and Grandma asked everyone to be seated, because dinner was all ready.

"Oh, I don't mind waiting a bit for dinner," said Constance, "if you all want to have cocktails first."

Grandma looked startled, and so did Dad. No one ever asked

for a drink at our house. "Oh, we never serve cocktails," Grandma said politely, and went on into the kitchen. Dad gave me a skeptical look behind Constance's back, and I hurriedly pulled out her chair.

"Miss Payne, you sit here," I said, covering the awkward moment.

"Please, Addie," she said. "Call me Constance."

Grandma brought in the plates, and we started eating and making small talk with Constance about how long it had been since she was in town and how busy she must be in New York. She seemed distracted and didn't really answer our questions about New York. I watched her closely, but I tried not to stare. I noticed she wasn't eating anything and was just pushing the food around on her plate.

"To think you turned out to be a famous star!" Grandma said to her. "I remember when you were just a little thing, reciting at the Sunday School pageants and all."

"Pass the salt, Addie," said Dad, sounding bored to death by all the chitchat.

"Were you in those things too?" I asked Constance. "So was I when I was little! I even wanted to be an actress then."

"Did you?" she asked, smiling at me.

"Yeah, once. Before I decided to be an artist."

"Addie, pass the pepper," Dad interrupted. He never had any patience with my ideas about being an artist.

I went on as though I hadn't heard him. "I'll probably study in Paris, and then when I'm famous, I'll live in New York."

I heard Dad give a little snort of derision.

"Yes," Constance said to me, "if you're going to be famous, New York is the place to be."

There was more small talk, and then Constance asked Grandma if there might be some wine. "Just a little touch," she said, "to go with the roast beef?"

I saw Grandma and Dad exchange a glance.

"I'm afraid there just isn't a thing in the way of spirits to be had in our house," Grandma answered. "We never partake."

Constance seemed embarrassed and rattled on about how she was used to taking wine with her meals and something about French wines coming back after the war, and we all looked at our plates awkwardly.

"Do you ever have champagne?" I asked, trying to rescue her from the silence. "I bet you have it on opening nights!"

"Oh, yes," she smiled, looking relieved. "That's a tradition."

"Oh, I wish we could see you on the stage! I wish you would at least do our style show!"

"Now don't go bothering her about that!" said Dad sharply.

"But couldn't you do it for old times' sake?" I continued. "I mean, you've never given a performance or anything in Clear River. People would like to see you."

"She doesn't want to be in some silly thing like that!" Dad said, annoyed. He turned to Constance. "I don't know where she gets these crazy ideas. She's always up to some nonsense— going to Paris and New York and wanting to be an artist!" He said it as though it were all quite ridiculous.

"Well, that's what I'm going to do!" I said angrily.

He turned back to me. "You'd better think about settling down somewhere and making a home for yourself, instead of doing so much daydreaming!"

I wanted to shout back at him, but I knew I mustn't, especially with company there.

Suddenly Constance spoke, looking right at him.

"Daydreaming isn't so bad," she said. "You have something to look forward to."

I was startled that she had come to my defense, and so was Dad. I felt his argument with me had somehow shifted to her.

"You look forward to gettin' a decent job," he said to her, "and making a living and trying to raise a family. That's about all there is."

"I guess that just isn't enough for some people," she said firmly, and they stared at each other almost angrily.

"Not for me," I said quietly.

Dad turned angrily back to me. "You'll find out when you grow up . . . and can't have everything you want!"

"It doesn't hurt to try for it!" I said defiantly.

For a moment he just stared at me, and I thought he was going to ask me to leave the table. Somehow Constance and I had joined forces against him, and he was furious.

Grandma was keeping out of it, but she cast me a sympathetic glance, and I knew she felt for me in moments like this. I was always full of daydreams that Dad thought were ridiculous, but she would understand and quietly encourage me.

There was silence for a few moments while we all ate. Then Constance suddenly spoke. "When is this style show of yours, Addie?"

"Next Wednesday," I said glumly.

"Well," she said, "maybe I can make it after all."

Dad gave her a sharp look as though she had said it just to annoy him.

"You mean it?" I asked excitedly.

"Yes, I think I can arrange it," she said, smiling.

I was astounded. My brainstorm had actually worked out!

"That's awful nice of you, Constance," said Grandma. "All the girls will be so excited."

"They'll run you ragged if you let 'em," Dad said to her scornfully.

"I'm sure they won't," she said politely, disagreeing with him again.

Suddenly Grandma and I realized the rolls were still in the oven and about to burn, and we ran to the kitchen. I was nervous about leaving Dad and Constance alone at the table, and I listened carefully from the kitchen to what they said.

There was an awkward silence, and then Dad made some small talk about being sorry to hear about her mother and how it had been a long time. There was another silence. Finally Dad spoke again.

"I remember how we used to tease you. We called you 'Countess Constance' because we thought you were stuck-up."

I couldn't believe he had said that to her. It seemed terribly rude, though I didn't think he had meant it that way.

"Yes. I remember," she said quietly, and I wondered if her feelings had been hurt by the memory of the other kids being unkind to her.

"Well," he said, a bit embarrassed and realizing he had sounded impolite, "I guess you showed everybody. You're the only one of us who made a big success."

Constance didn't reply, and I rushed back in with the rolls before they could get into another disagreement.

Constance seemed more nervous than ever and looked at her

watch and said she really had to leave and get her call from New York. I had never known anybody in Clear River who had a long distance call from New York City, and the idea seemed very glamorous to me. She got up from the table abruptly and started for the door. I was startled that anyone would get up and leave in the middle of one of Grandma's roast beef dinners, and I tried to convince her to stay for dessert. She seemed very agitated and insisted she had to go. As she rushed out the door, I called after her to remind her of the style show, and she promised she would be there.

As I came back in, I saw that she had forgotten her gloves. I picked them up and hurried to the door and called after her, but she had already gone. Dad and Grandma had sat back down at the table and were talking quietly about how upset Constance had seemed. I went to put her gloves in the desk drawer, and as I smoothed them out, I found myself trying one of them on. When I slipped my hand into it, I realized it was very old and worn, and my finger poked up through the end of it. I stared at the glove and wondered why a famous star like Constance would wear something so old and shabby.

The afternoon of the style show luncheon, Carla Mae, Gloria, Tanya and I carefully carried our dresses to the Dew Drop Inn. The Inn was the only restaurant in Clear River, and it had a dining room that was often the scene of town social functions.

We had been writing and rewriting our narration for days and figured we were as close as we would ever get to putting on a real Paris-type fashion show like the ones we saw in the newsreels.

I was feeling triumphant. All the ladies were dying to see Constance, and it had been my idea to invite her. Her appearance would be the high point of the afternoon. The ladies had finished their luncheon, and the show was about to begin. A panel of the Women's Club would judge our creations, and Constance would award the prizes. A chair had been reserved for her at the end of the head table so that she could arrive just as the show began. But I noticed she still wasn't there.

Mrs. Tuttle, who played the organ in our church on Sundays, was there to play the piano for the style show, and Mrs. Coyne, who owned the Dew Drop Inn, would narrate. As each of us came out on the little stage, we would hand our card to Mrs. Coyne and she would read it, dramatically describing the details of our dresses.

We milled around nervously backstage while the first few girls went out. We kept peeking out the door to see how the ladies were responding to the show and looking to see if Constance had arrived yet. Her chair was still empty.

Carla Mae was on next, in her pink dress with ruffles all over it. I had told her I thought it was a little too dippy with all those ruffles, but it was the kind of thing she liked. She walked nervously up and down the "runway" aisle and swooshed around a couple of times so everybody could see her ruffles as Mrs. Coyne read her card.

"Miss Carla Mae Carter in her original creation, 'Pink Parfait,' " Mrs. Coyne read. "A lovely number to wear to a Hollywood premiere at Grauman's Chinese Theatre or for eating caviar and champagne at the Eiffel Tower. Yards and yards of fluffy ruffles in strawberry pink provide just the right feminine touch for today's young lady . . . 'Pink Parfait.' "

I thought that was a particularly icky description, and I thought I saw Mrs. Coyne trying to hide a smile as she read it.

Then Gloria came out in her dress. It was bright green plaid with white cuffs, white trim around the hem, white belt, white collar and a gigantic white bow at the chin. Unfortunately, Gloria had made the bow so enormous that she had to tilt her head back to keep from ruining the bow, and she had a little trouble seeing where she was going. As a result, she came leaning down the aisle as though she were descending a steep hill. Besides, she hated the whole idea of walking out in front of all those people, so she rushed up and down the aisle like the place was on fire, and she was off stage before Mrs. Coyne had a chance to finish reading her card. All the ladies laughed and applauded her anyway.

When Gloria came off, the four of us poked our heads out the door again to see if Constance had arrived. She hadn't.

"What are we going to do if she doesn't show?" asked Carla Mae.

"She'll be here!" I said, trying to sound positive. "She'll be here! Just don't panic!"

"Well, what if she doesn't come in time to give out the awards?" asked Tanya. "You and your big ideas!"

"Oh, zip your lip, Smithers," I said irritably.

We heard Mrs. Coyne introducing Tanya next, and she made her way to the stage. Her dress was as obnoxious as she was. She imagined herself a great ballerina, and her dress was a sort of draped chiffon affair in sea-foam green. She had a big bunch of artificial flowers pinned at the waist and actually had the nerve to wear ballet shoes. She was covered in all her mother's best rhinestone jewelry. I had told her that she looked like some-body's fairy godmother, but she just sniffed and said I had no idea of high class and elegance.

She walked up and down the aisle in a slow-step, as though she were in a wedding procession, and then suddenly, with a great lunge, pirouetted around like a top, then went back to her slow-step. She was absolutely ridiculous. Her narration, of course, was the ickiest of them all.

"Next is Miss Tanya Smithers, in her creation for the artistic young woman, 'Green Goddess.' Note the classical Greek lines in the drape of the luxurious fabric." As Mrs. Coyne read Tanya moved her hands over her dress to demonstrate. "And the lovely way the dress moves on the graceful dancer's form." I could tell it was all Mrs. Coyne could do to keep from laughing as she read what Tanya had written. "A perfect frock for sitting in the Royal Box at the opera, or for waltzing in the Vienna woods, or for a New York penthouse cocktail party . . . 'Green Goddess.'"

Tanya kept on posing and pirouetting, even after Mrs. Coyne had finished with her narration, and Mrs. Coyne practically had to ask her to get off the stage.

"That was absolutely revolting!" I said to Tanya, when she came off stage. She just stuck her nose in the air and pranced by us, quite satisfied with herself.

"You're next, Addie!" hissed Carla Mae.

"OK, I'm going!" I answered.

"My gosh," said Gloria, "Constance still isn't here!"

"Don't worry!" I said, and ran for the stage.

I wasn't too crazy about parading up and down in front of the whole Women's Club like a heifer at the County Fair, so I shoved my card into Mrs. Coyne's hand and shot up and down the aisle rather stiffly, trying to get the ordeal over with as quickly as possible. Grandma was in the audience, and she caught my eye and smiled.

My secret dress design was bright blue with red and white rickrack everywhere. I just loved rickrack, and I had gone absolutely crazy trimming the dress. It looked like a road map. As I whirred by, Mrs. Coyne read the description I had written on my card.

" 'Rickrack Rhapsody,' by Adelaide Mills . . . the perfect dress for driving in your European sports car or signing autographs at Hollywood and Vine or perhaps for brunching in the Blue Room at the White House." I thought that was one of the better lines of my narration, tying in the color of the dress and the Blue Room and all.

"Note the unusual detailing in the application of rickrack," Mrs. Coyne continued. "On the sleeves, on the cuffs, on the collar . . ." As she mentioned each part of the dress, I gestured with my hands to show it to the judges. I had rehearsed it a dozen times at home, but in the heat of the moment I forgot what order the details came in, and I ended up frantically waving my hands around like a windmill, trying to follow what Mrs. Coyne was reading from my card. "On the bodice, on the skirt, on the hem . . ." She began to laugh, but continued reading, "On the socks, on the purse, on the pigtails . . ." At that the whole audience began to laugh. "On the hat, indeed, a veritable 'Rickrack Rhapsody.' "

Suddenly, the door opened at the end of the room, and there was a terrbile crash. Constance had come in and had swung the

door open too hard, knocking over a tray of dishes. Everything stopped, and there was an awkward silence.

"Excuse me," she said. "Didn't mean to interrupt."

Then one of the judges motioned Constance to her seat at the head table, and Mrs. Coyne finished with my narration. Constance nodded in my direction as she sat down, and I could see she was sorry for spoiling my big moment in front of the judges. I went quickly off the stage, embarrassed at the commotion.

I had been the last to show my dress, and we were all called out on the stage again to wait for the judges' decision. Everyone in the restaurant was watching Constance, and she seemed self-conscious. She was wearing a pale blue suit and a dramatic brown hat with pheasant feathers. She lit up a cigarette and fiddled with it nervously as the judges handed their decision to Mrs. Coyne.

Mrs. Coyne gave Constance a flowery introduction and said, "Won't you please give a warm welcome to our own Broadway star, Miss Constance Payne!"

The audience applauded, but Constance didn't seem to realize she was supposed to go up on the stage until one of the judges next to her tapped her shoulder. She looked startled, then got up suddenly and accidently pushed her chair against the foot of a lady seated behind her. The woman let out a cry of pain, and Constance seemed flustered and fumbled for a place to put out her cigarette. She walked up the steps to the stage and stumbled slightly at the top. The whole audience gasped.

"I'm used to coming out from the wings," Constance said nervously, "not up the steps." There was a slight ripple of laughter from the audience. All of us on the stage were watching Constance closely. I wondered why a big star like her would be so nervous and clumsy in front of a crowd.

Mrs. Coyne handed her the paper with the winners' names, and Constance stared at it blankly for a long moment.

"Oh," she said, "I forgot my glasses." She started digging through her purse.

"Can I help?" asked Mrs. Coyne.

"No, no, no. It's all right," Constance said. She looked out at the audience apologetically. "I know how excited . . ."

"Louder please!" someone called from the back of the room.

Constance began again, louder. "I know how excited you all are to hear the winners . . ." She trailed off without finishing the sentence, still searching in her purse. I stared at her, wondering what was wrong and why she was so inept. I had expected her to be dazzling.

"I think she's drunk!" someone near the stage whispered loudly. We all heard it, and I looked quickly over at Constance. She had heard it too. She looked as though her face had been slapped. I realized that the woman in the audience was right. I suddenly felt sick. I wanted to be anywhere but there. It had been my idea to invite Constance, and now it was a mess and all my fault. I wished she had never said yes. She went on fumbling in her purse, looking for her glasses.

"Wait," she said. "This'll just take me a minute."

"I'll be glad to read the names for you," said Mrs. Coyne, reaching for the piece of paper.

"I'm sorry," said Constance. "Just a moment."

I was burning with embarrassment for her, and I could feel the discomfort from everyone else on stage. I knew drunk people could be unpredictable, and I was afraid she might do something awful.

"I'm afraid the handwriting's hard to read," said Mrs. Coyne, tugging at the paper. "Let me help you."

"No, it's all right," said Constance. And suddenly, as they pulled in opposite directions, the paper tore in half, and Constance's purse dropped from her arm and its contents spilled out on the floor. There was a titter, then cold silence from the audience.

Constance knelt unsteadily to try and gather up her belongings, and Mrs. Coyne, trying to make the best of an awkward situation, bent to help her.

Then Constance seemed to give up and whispered to Mrs. Coyne, "I think you'd better do it. I'm afraid I'm just not feeling very well."

"Of course," said Mrs. Coyne.

Constance grabbed her purse, leaving some of her things on the floor, and turned to leave.

"Excuse me . . . you'll have to excuse me," she said in the direction of the audience. Then her eyes met mine. She looked terribly sad, and turned and walked quickly to the door. There was a deadly silence as everyone turned to watch her pass by. When she reached the door, she fumbled with the knob, and all eyes were on her as she struggled to get out of the room.

I wondered at that moment, why, in the movies, drunk people were always funny—staggering and hiccuping. Constance wasn't funny at all. I stood on the stage, watching the door after she left, not even listening when Mrs. Coyne announced Mary Beth Walsh had won first prize. I didn't care.

Chapter Four

GRANDMA AND I DIDN'T SAY much to each other on the way home from the style show. She always knew when I didn't feel like talking, and she would let me keep my silence for a while. Sooner or later she would encourage me to talk it out, but I appreciated just being left alone sometimes, and she understood.

We weren't home long when Mrs. Coyne arrived with the things from Constance's purse that had been left behind. She said that she knew I was a friend of Constance's and that it might be better if I took the things to her because Constance might be embarrassed to see her. I thought it was good of Mrs. Coyne to realize that, but then she was one of nicest people I knew. She said she and Constance had been friends in school and that she had always liked and admired her. Grandma told me not to blame myself for what had happened, but it didn't cheer me up much. I just sat there after Mrs. Coyne left and stared at Constance's sunglasses and the other things she had left behind.

Dad came home soon, carrying a bunch of pussywillows he had found near the gravel pit where he was working. Usually I would have been delighted, but I was too glum to care. He knew what had happened at the style show. He had heard the story from someone when he had stopped at the post office on the way home, and he said it was all over town by now.

"The whole thing doesn't surprise me a bit," he said. "That's about what I'd expect from old Constance."

"Now, James!" said Grandma. "You shouldn't say those things."

"Oh, Mother!" he said. "Her dad was a boozer, and she takes after him. Remember how she was looking for a drink over here at dinner the other night?"

"Well," said Grandma, "there's lots of folks take a drink at dinner and don't go overboard with it. It's just too bad she don't know how to handle it. I feel kinda sorry for her."

"Me, too," I said.

"Boy!" Dad laughed. "She must've been some sight! Lurching around."

"James!" said Grandma.

"There wasn't anything funny about it!" I said angrily. I was almost surprised to find myself defending Constance after what she had done. I was puzzled about what had happened. I didn't understand why she would drink too much before setting off for such an important event, knowing that people would be watching her closely.

"Sure wasn't funny," said Grandma. "I bet she must feel awful about what she did."

"I'll bet she's done the same thing a dozen times before," said Dad. "People get hittin' the bottle, and they don't care what anybody thinks. And going around feeling sorry for 'em only makes 'em worse."

"How do *you* know?" I asked angrily.

"I've seen plenty of 'em," he said. "Old George Bardle used to drink on the job all the time. He'd go on a toot and then come whinin' around sayin' he was sorry, and they'd give him another chance and a couple of days later he'd be off again. People like that never change."

"Anybody can change, James, if they get the chance," said Grandma. "Poor old George didn't have a friend in the world."

"What do you expect when somebody behaves like that?" asked Dad.

"Well," Grandma said, almost to herself. "It's too bad Constance don't have someone to help her out."

After supper that night, Gloria, Tanya and Carla Mae came over, and we spread ourselves out around the kitchen table to do our egg-decorating. We dipped hard-boiled eggs in dye water and put decals and ink designs on them. We used our hollowed-out eggshells for more permanent decorating jobs. My grandmother always kept bits of trimming and buttons in old Quaker Oats boxes, and we had three of these big round boxes of treasures on the table.

We took out bits of velvet ribbon and rickrack and fancy buttons, and carefully glued them to the hollow eggs in various patterns. I made a red, white and blue rickrack egg that matched my Easter Style Show dress, just to drive everybody crazy.

While we worked, we discussed the relative merits of each other's egg designs and then got to the subject we were really dying to discuss, Constance Payne. We talked in low, furtive tones, so Dad and Grandma couldn't hear us from the living room.

"Well," said Tanya. "Her name is absolutely *dirt* in this town from now on! My mother says she should be ridden out of town on a rail!"

"Oh, what does your mother know? She's never had the problems of a great dramatic actress!" I said angrily.

"Just because she's an actress," said Tanya, "is no reason to get drunk!"

"I felt sorry for her," said Gloria.

"Me too," said Carla Mae. "It was so embarrassing."

"I did too," I said. "My grandmother says she probably needs help."

"Yeah," said Tanya. "She needed some help getting the door open to get out of there."

"Smithers, you have absolutely no human compassion!" I said haughtily.

"She's just an old lush!" said Tanya.

"Great artists have problems other people can't understand," I said. "Remember how Van Gogh cut off his own ear?"

"Yeccch," said Gloria.

"If you ever really get to be a prima ballerina, Tanya," I continued, "you'll probably be a dope fiend or a split personality or something."

"Ha!" said Tanya.

"Yeah," said Carla Mae. "You'll probably be dancing around in a padded cell!"

"In a 'Green Goddess' strait jacket," said Gloria, and she cracked her gum furiously, right in Tanya's ear. Carla Mae and

I cracked ours too, and Tanya clamped her hands over her ears with an anguished expression.

"Now, listen," I said, when the frantic chewing had stopped. "I have this fantastic idea for a project for all of us."

They all stared at me expectantly. I was notorious for having brilliant brainstorms.

I waited for an appropriately dramatic pause. "I think we should all get Constance Payne to give us dramatic lessons!"

There was stunned silence for a moment.

"You're out of your mind!" hissed Tanya. "What do we need with dramatic lessons?"

"Listen," I said, trying to sound very logical. "Didn't we agree in our New Year's resolutions that we were gonna do all kinds of self-improvement stuff? And now it's almost Easter, and what have we done? Not one, single, solitary project!"

"I take dancing lessons every week," said Tanya haughtily.

"We know, we know!" said Carla Mae. "You've been doing that for years, so that's not an *improvement* for this year."

"Well," said Tanya, "I don't see how dramatic lessons are going to improve me. I don't want to be an actress."

"Great dancers are supposed to be dramatic on the stage," I said. "It would probably help you a lot—later in your ballet career." I winked at Carla Mae and she smirked. Tanya's pretensions as a great ballerina were a running joke among the rest of us.

"I bet it's expensive, though," said Gloria.

"We can collect pop bottles and stuff to raise the money," I said. "I don't think it would cost more than fifty cents each. I think that's what we should offer."

"That's a lot," said Gloria.

"Yeah, but we'll only take a few lessons, because she won't be here that long."

"I don't know," said Gloria.

"Oh, come on!" I said impatiently. "Everybody give me fifty cents tomorrow, and I'll go and see her after lunch."

"I don't know," said Tanya. "Fifty cents?"

"Yeah," said Carla Mae, "that's expensive . . . and after what happened at the style show and everything."

I knew one last thing I could do to get them to agree. I spit on my hand and held it out to them. That was the signal for our secret oath, and they couldn't go back on it. They all hesitated for a moment.

"Is it a pact?" I asked, and started to chant the oath. "Faithful friends through thick and thin, if we lose or if we win . . ."

I stared at the three of them, and one by one, they reluctantly joined in, spitting on their palms and reaching across the table to shake hands in unison as we continued the oath.

"Signed in blood and sealed in spit, our loyalty will never quit. Cross your heart and hope to die, stick a needle in your eye. Vow to keep the secret code, or turn into an ugly toad!"

The next day I rode over to Constance's house on my bike, taking along the things from her purse. I couldn't resist trying on her sunglasses. I had never owned a pair of sunglasses, and I felt terribly glamorous and mysterious in them. I put them on right over my own glasses and wore both pair as I pedaled down the street. I took them off before I knocked on her door, because I didn't want her to think I was making fun of her.

I had approached Gloria and Carla Mae and Tanya with the idea that the dramatic lessons would be good for the four of us, but I was also thinking of it as a project to take Constance's mind off her drinking and give her some company. We would be helping to save a great star. I didn't know what to expect when she came to the door. She was barefoot, and her hair was a bit disheveled. She was wearing her black and red kimono again. When she saw me, she looked embarrassed.

"Hi!" I said brightly, as though nothing had happened.

"Hi," she said softly.

I handed her the things, and she took them, giving me an apologetic look. "Come on in," she said. "I . . . I just wasn't feeling very well yesterday . . ."

"I know," I interrupted. "I mean, it's OK. It was just a dumb style show."

"Thank you for not being angry," she said, and she put her arm around my shoulder as we walked into the living room.

As soon as we sat down, I launched into my request about the acting lessons, telling her that we would really appreciate it very much to have a chance to be exposed to someone artistic like her.

She looked startled, then laughed an odd laugh and said she didn't think she was the kind of teacher we ought to have, and anyway, she had to get back to New York.

I was very disappointed at her refusal. "Boy," I sighed, "I wish I was going with you. I hate it here sometimes."

"You don't know how lucky you are to live in Clear River," she said. "New York can be a terrible place!"

"I bet I'd love it!" I said.

She smiled. "You probably would."

I realized then that she really understood. She was the only person I had ever mentioned my daydreams of New York to who didn't seem opposed to the idea. She actually knew that I was serious, and she knew I'd like it.

"Maybe you'll get to go someday," she said.

"Not if my dad has anything to say about it," I said. "He thinks I should get married or be a schoolteacher or something. He never wants me to do anything that's exciting!"

"Well, parents are like that. They worry about you. They want you to be safe. My parents were the same way. They didn't want me to go on the stage."

"That would have been awful!" I said. "Think what you would have missed! You couldn't have been a famous actress if you'd stayed here."

"Well," she said, "there are other things in life . . ."

"That's what Dad always says, every time I talk about being an artist or going to Paris or New York. He acts like it's going to the moon or something!"

"He just wants you to be happy."

"Staying here wouldn't make me happy in a million years," I said. "I mean, I like it, but I just don't want to sit around here and do nothing for the rest of my life! I want to see what's going on in the world! I want to visit every country and eat every kind of food and see every museum and read every book and do something that's never been done before! I don't want to be like everybody else!"

I stopped, amazed at myself making that big speech to her. I realized that even though I didn't know Constance very well,

I had told her a lot of things I had never discussed with anyone else. I think she knew that.

She looked at me quietly for a moment and then she said, "I guess I owe you *something* for what happened yesterday. If you really want me to give you a lesson, I will."

"You mean it?" I said, excited.

"Sure," she smiled.

I jumped up and gave her a big hug, then pulled out the two dollars in change we had collected and dumped it on the table in front of the sofa. I said I knew it wasn't much, but it was all we could afford for the first lesson, and she could teach us all at once in a group. She tried to give the money back to me and said she wouldn't charge us, but I insisted and said we wanted it to be strictly professional.

I said we would be there at four that afternoon and ran out before she could change her mind again.

Chapter Five

AT FOUR THAT AFTERNOON, we were in Constance Payne's living room, ready to become great dramatic actresses. She was dressed in a plain blue suit with a white blouse, and she had brushed her hair back neatly and put on makeup. I had been afraid that she wouldn't take us seriously as students, but on the contrary, she talked to us about acting with great intensity and seemed to believe we really wanted to learn.

We had all been prepared to start out with a big death scene or something equally dramatic from the latest Broadway hit, but much to our surprise she asked us to do something that sounded like a children's game to us.

Carla Mae and I were to pretend that there was a big spring dance approaching and that I was trying to get Carla Mae to double-date with me. I would go with my favorite boy and she with hers, and the object was for Carla Mae to hesitate to accept and for me to insist on it.

Constance called this "improvisation," and it seemed rather silly to us . . . just playing "let's pretend" like little kids. But just before we started, she whispered something to Carla Mae that the rest of us couldn't hear. Then she told us to behave just as we would if the circumstances were real, to talk to each other as we usually did.

Carla Mae and I began our imaginary conversation.

"Hi!" I said, not quite sure how to start. "Heard about the big spring dance next week?"

"Yeah," Carla Mae answered. "Sounds neat."

"I'm gonna invite Billy Wild, so you wanna double-date, you and Delmer Doakes?"

The others giggled when I mentioned the boys Carla Mae and I liked the best.

"No, thanks," she answered.

"How come?"

"I just don't want to, that's all."

"Well, why not?" I asked.

"I just don't."

"Well, you have to have a reason."

"Says who?"

"We always do everything together," I said. "Why wouldn't we go to the dance together?"

"Well," she said slyly, "maybe I've made other plans."

"What other plans?"

"Never mind."

"What is this?" I asked, getting annoyed. "We have a pact not to keep secrets from each other!"

"This is different," she said.

"Why is it different?"

"You'll find out," she said smugly.

"Well, that's just dumb! Why can't you tell me?"

"I just don't want to," she said.

I was losing my temper. "This is just dumb!" I said, turning to Constance. "We're supposed to talk to each other like we really do, but she would never do that."

"Are you sure?" asked Constance, smiling a bit.

"Yeah," I said, not really very sure at all.

"Keep trying," said Constance. "Maybe you'll find out what's going on."

I turned back to Carla Mae. "OK!" I shouted right in her face. "Once and for all, what's going on?"

"I'm not telling," she said frostily, and sat on the edge of the sofa. The others were snickering.

"All right for you!" I said. "You can just forget about being my best friend."

"Fine!" she retorted.

"This is really stupid!" I said, leaning over her and trying to intimidate her. "I don't see how we're supposed to do this scene if you don't cooperate!"

"Well, I *am* cooperating!" she shouted, rising and trying to tower over me. "Constance told me to pretend I already invited your boyfriend myself, and I didn't want you to find out about it. That's why I wouldn't go and wouldn't tell why."

Tanya and Gloria howled with laughter, and I groaned and flopped down on the sofa.

Constance laughed. "Now, did that argument seem real to you?" she asked.

Everybody agreed that it had.

"Why do you think it seemed real?" she asked.

"Because," I said, still burned at being tricked. "She really was keeping a secret from me, and it made me mad."

"Right," said Constance. "You weren't just playing 'let's pretend.' You were really arguing, yet you were doing it in pretend circumstances. Understand?"

"I guess so," said Gloria, sounding vague.

"You don't *act* something," Constance said. "You *do* something. You do something *real* in imaginary circumstances."

Suddenly I understood what she was talking about, and my anger evaporated. "I get it!" I said excitedly. "That's neat!"

We were all fascinated with the illustration she had just given us, and I began to believe that there was a lot more to acting than I had ever imagined.

Constance then set up an improvisation for Tanya and Gloria, in which Gloria would describe a new boy she liked, and Tanya would disagree. It worked out very well, with Tanya getting all hot under the collar about how awful the boy was, and Gloria defending him until Tanya tried to end it by pointing out that he wasn't even a real person, just imaginary. Gloria shut her up by asking if he was only imaginary, then why was Tanya arguing about him. That sent us all into a fit of giggles, and Constance told them they had done very well.

"I didn't know acting was so easy," said Gloria.

"Well, it isn't really," said Constance, smiling.

"Yeah," I said. "We're just making up our own lines so it seems real. What do you do when you hafta read someone else's lines?"

"Yeah," said Carla Mae. "Like Shakespeare, that's so hard!"

"Well," said Constance, "it's really the same thing."

"What do you mean?" asked Gloria.

"Well, you were trying to tell Tanya how much you liked the new boy," said Constance. "How handsome he was—that he was neat and cute and a sharp dresser. And it's the same thing when you're doing something in Shakespeare."

She paused for a moment, thinking of an example.

"For instance," she went on, "Cleopatra says that Antony's 'face was as the heavens; and therein stuck a sun and moon, which kept their course and lighted the little O, the earth.'"

We were all watching her intently. None of us knew anything about Shakespeare, because in Clear River you didn't study that until you got into high school, but we knew who Cleopatra was, and we were fascinated with what she had to say about Antony.

"'His legs bestrid the ocean,'" Constance continued. "'His rear'd arm crested the world. His voice was propertied as all the tuned spheres, and that to friends; but when he meant to quail and shake the orb, he was as rattling thunder.'"

She said it fiercely, and we watched wide-eyed. She seemed really caught up in it, and I could actually imagine Cleopatra talking about Antony. Certainly Constance was only acting, but somehow what she was saying seemed more real than any of our "improvisation."

"'For his bounty,'" she went on, "'there was no winter in't; an autumn 'twas that grew the more by reaping: his delights were dolphin-like; they show'd his back above the element they lived in: in his livery walk'd crowns and crownets; realms and islands were as plates dropp'd from his pocket. Think you there was, or might be, such a man as this I dream'd of? . . . if there be, or ever were, one such, it's past the size of dreaming. . .'"

When she had finished, she looked over at us almost as though she had forgotten we were there. We had been spellbound.

I wasn't quite sure what all the words had meant, but I

knew that I had just heard something very special and moving. She was the first real actor I had ever seen, and the experience of watching her become another person in front of my eyes was something I would never forget. I sensed that Constance had within her that same creative secret that I would have to uncover in myself if I were ever going to be a real artist.

The next day, we trooped back to Constance's house for our second lesson. We were all caught up in the thrill of being actresses. I had been practicing at home in front of the mirror, trying to walk like Constance and trying to copy her British accent. I wrapped my old blue chenille bathrobe around me and swept dramatically up and down my bedroom, pretending I was wearing her black and red kimono.

She didn't answer when we knocked on the door, and we wondered if she had forgotten that we were coming. Finally, I realized that the door was open, and we went in. We called out to her, but there was no answer.

We tiptoed quietly down the dark hall, thinking she might be asleep, and peered cautiously into the living room. Constance was lying on the sofa, and a bottle of liquor and a glass sat on the table in front of her.

"Hi," I said tentatively.

For a moment, she didn't stir, then she turned her head and looked at us. She looked bleary-eyed and pale, as though she were exhausted. "What are you doing here?" she asked.

"It's time for our lesson," I said.

"Go on home," she said irritably. "Haven't got anything to teach." She started to sit up and lost her balance, almost falling off the edge of the sofa. She put her hand out toward the table to steady herself.

"She's drunk as a skunk!" Tanya said in a loud whisper.

"Shut up!" I said, knowing Constance had heard. I turned back to Constance. "Are you sure you're all right?"

"Just go away!" she said angrily.

"C'mon, Addie!" said Carla Mae. "She's drunk! Let's get out of here."

"Oh, go on!" I said to her, and the three girls all ran quickly to the front door and left.

Constance seemed unaware that I was still there. She reached for a cigarette and sat slumped on the sofa as she lit it. She held the match in her hand a moment too long until it burned her fingers, and she dropped it quickly.

I ran over to her. "Are you all right?"

I had startled her, and she turned angrily toward me.

"Leave me alone!" she said.

"I was just trying to help," I said. "Maybe I should fix you some coffee or something."

"Coffee!" she said sarcastically. "I don't need coffee, I need another drink." She took the bottle and started to pour more liquor into her glass. I could tell she really wanted to be left alone, but I wasn't sure I should go. I felt it wasn't right to just leave her there like that.

I reached for the bottle and tried gently to pull it back from her.

"Let go!" she said.

"But you're sick . . . you can't drink any more," I said, and desperately tried to pull it out of her hands.

For a second we struggled with the bottle, then suddenly she thrust it toward me. "Take the damn thing!" she shouted, and it slipped out of my hands and shattered on the floor.

"Look what you've done!" she shouted. "You stupid little brat!" Her remark hurt me, but I knew she was not herself.

"I didn't mean to." I said quietly, and tried to pick up some of the pieces of the broken bottle.

She moved away from me and stood near the fireplace with her back to me. "You shouldn't be nosing around here anyway," she said angrily.

"We came for our lessons," I reminded her. "You told us to come at three."

"Lessons!" she said sarcastically. "I could give lessons for a hundred years, and it wouldn't make any difference!"

"You said we were doing good!" I replied, hurt by her remark.

"Good?" She laughed harshly. "It's pathetic! Not an ounce of talent . . . couldn't get a job sweeping the stage!"

She seemed nervous and very distraught, almost out of control. It scared me, but somehow I knew from the tone of her voice that she was just rambling on and that I shouldn't pay attention to what she was saying. I moved toward her. I thought maybe I could convince her to lie down or eat something.

"Constance," I said.

"Go away!" she said, her back still to me. She said it in a weary voice, pleading with me to leave her by herself.

I reached out to touch her shoulder.

"Leave me alone, you scrawny little brat!" She turned on me suddenly and threw her drink right into my face.

I was so stunned that for a moment I just stood there, frozen to the spot, liquor running down my face and stinging my eyes. She stood staring at me, empty glass in her hand, as though she couldn't believe what she had just done.

Then I turned and started to run for the door. Halfway across the room, I turned back to her. "I'd rather be a scrawny brat than an old drunk!" I said, near tears. Then I ran out the front door. As I fled down the steps, I heard her call my name, but I didn't turn back.

I ran all the way home and burst in the kitchen door. Grandma was baking my favorite chocolate cake, and ordinarily that would have diverted me from almost anything. This time, though, I just threw myself down in a chair and started to cry all over the kitchen table. Grandma stopped beating her cake batter and wiped her hands on her apron and came over to me. "For heavens' sake, what's the matter, Addie?" she asked.

I tearfully told her what had happened and said that I hated Constance and thought she was the most awful person I had ever met.

"She was like a witch!" I said.

"Now, Addie," said Grandma. "I don't want to hear talk like that. Even if you've got a right to be mad, don't go sayin' mean things."

"I was just trying to help her, and she blew her top! It was awful!"

"Well," Grandma said, going back to mixing her cake. "I guess she can't help herself."

"She was so nice to us yesterday when we had our first lesson.

Today she was like a different person. I think she's crazy!"

"Drinkin' can make people crazy."

"Then why do they do it?" I asked angrily.

"Well, I suppose they got somethin' they just can't face up to, and liquor helps 'em forget for a while."

"I just couldn't believe she was so mean."

"You mustn't let such a thing hurt your feelin's. You just remember that Constance must be hurtin' a lot worse than you to go and behave like that."

I knew that Grandma was probably right, but I was too angry to feel charitable. "I think Dad was right," I said. "She's just trash!"

"Now I don't want to hear talk like that. Your Dad's pretty smart, but he gets some funny ideas sometimes. He don't show much sympathy for weakness, and he can't understand people who don't walk the straight and narrow just like him . . ."

"Well," I interrupted angrily. "Nobody should behave like her!"

"It ain't right to go around judgin' other people's lives," Grandma continued. "That's the Lord's business and not ours. You have to learn to be a little forgiving. You can dislike what a person does and still like the person."

"I wouldn't ever go near her again!"

"Well," she said quietly, "maybe you ought not to. But it'd sure be a pity if she didn't have any friends at all."

There was something about Grandma's insistence on seeing the good in people that could be very irritating. Just when you were ready for anger and revenge, she would remind you that it was pointless, and you'd have to figure out some other solution.

I was so angry at Constance that I wasn't ready to give in to positive feelings yet.

"Well, you said before she needed a friend," I argued. "And I was her friend, and look where it got me! Some friend!"

"I know," she answered. "Sometimes bein' friends is hard work. But a true friend don't give up on somebody when things go wrong. You try to help out."

"Dad says it doesn't do any good. People like her never change anyway."

"I think anybody can change," Grandma said. "Why I was in my sixties when your momma died, and I came to live with you and your dad and started raisin' a family all over again. It was a big change in my life, but I did it, and it turned out fine."

"But you weren't living a bad life," I said, still arguing.

"Well, if your life is bad, then all the more reason you might want to start over fresh," she said. "It's like things comin' up again in the spring—that's really what Easter is all about—the promise of a new life. Spring is like the Lord's tryin' to show us that there's always hope, and there's always a chance for a new life. You see?"

"Yeah, I guess so," I said. She had given me so much to think about that I wasn't sure what I thought. Grandma was hard to argue with when it came to the subject of right and wrong. She had been working it out for some seventy years, and she was pretty sure which was which by now.

I was angry and hurt, but I couldn't forget all the good feelings I had had about Constance when we first met. I couldn't forget how much I liked her, and I tried to figure out what to do about it.

"Well, don't you brood about it," Grandma said, getting up from the table and handing me the cake bowl. "Here, you beat this thirty more strokes . . . that'll take your mind off your troubles."

She busied herself with something at the sink, and I sat there beating the cake batter furiously and counting the strokes to myself under my breath. But I was thinking about what Grandma had said about anybody being able to change.

"Do you think Constance would ever do that?" I asked. "Start over . . . a new life?"

"I don't know," said Grandma. "It's pretty hard when you're alone."

I thought about Constance a lot for the rest of the day.

Chapter Six

BY THE FOLLOWING MORNING, I had decided to make one more try to get through to Constance. I didn't like what she had done, but I knew she had tried to be friends with me—coming to dinner and to the style show and giving us that wonderful first acting lesson. I thought I owed her something for that.

I needed Dad to help me with my plan, so I decided to go out and visit him on his job. I often did that when I was on vacation from school. The big gravel pit where he loaded the trucks with his crane was only a mile from town, and I would ride my bike out and take him some special treat to add to his lunch. He would let me climb up in the cab of the crane with him and let me work the levers, and we would talk and then eat together. He always pretended that I was kind of in the way, but I think he liked having me come out and visit him.

I gave him a super-loud whistle through my teeth as I pulled up on my bike, and he waved at me from the machine. He put the big engine into neutral so he could shout down to me from the cab. "What are you up to?" he asked.

"Brought you some cold lemonade and some chocolate cake for an afternoon snack. Grandma forgot to pack the cake for you this morning."

"Boy!" he said. "You must want somethin' pretty big . . . comin' all the way out here with cake and lemonade." Sometimes he could just about read my mind, which I found a big disadvantage. I wondered if he could guess what my plan was and why I had come to see him.

"Well," I said, "I get some cake too."

"Yeah," he replied. "I thought there was a catch to the deal."

"It's only fair! I helped make it," I said, and climbed up into the cab of the machine with him.

"Well," he said, "I paid for it." He said that a lot around our house.

"That's your job," I said, not wanting to hear his usual tirade about money. "To pay for stuff."

"You're tellin' me," he said sarcastically. "I wouldn't be sittin' on this thing if I didn't have to."

"I like it!"

"Try it eight hours a day, and you won't like it so much."

He was right about that. I had once decided I wanted to be a crane operator when I grew up and spent a whole day with him on a job. It was too hot and dirty and noisy for me, and at the end of the day I had decided on another career. I enjoyed being on the machine for an hour or so, but I wondered how he could stand it every day for all those years. I had much more respect for the work he did after that day I spent with him, and I knew that his job wasn't the fun it looked to be. I also knew he was very good at it and was proud of his skill with the big machine. I liked that about him.

"Let me run it for a minute, huh?" I asked.

"No, I want to stop and have my lemonade."

"Oh, come on, just for a minute, just one bucketful?"

"OK," he said, sounding irritated. "We'll fill up that one hopper over there." I think he was secretly pleased that I liked working the machine.

He put the machine into gear and helped me pull the big levers to scoop up a bucketful of gravel. Then we hauled it up into the air and swung the boom over to the hopper and opened the bucket to dump the gravel. Later a big gravel truck would drive under the hopper and pull a lever that would empty just the right amount into the truck.

"OK, that's enough," he said.

"That was neat!" I said. "I love the way it takes a big bite out of the pile of gravel . . ."

"Come on, now," he said, climbing down out of the cab. "Let's eat. I can only take a few minutes. I'm busy as the devil."

"How do you know how busy the devil is?" I asked, climbing down with him.

"Know him personally," he said.

"Yeah? What does he look like?"

"Oh, about twelve years old, pigtails, glasses . . ."

"Oh, very funny!" I said. That was a typical Dad joke— always poking a bit of fun at me to get a laugh. Most of the time he was funny, but once in a while he hurt my feelings. I seldom let on though, because I knew he didn't mean to.

I poured the lemonade, then took a giant bite of my cake.

He looked at me and shook his head. "Your teeth are going to fall out one of these days! The way you eat sweets!"

I stretched my lips over my teeth and gave him a fake tooth- less smile. He did just what I knew he would do. He suddenly shoved his false upper plate of teeth out at me and made a grotesque face. I squealed in disgust as I always did, and he slid his teeth back in and laughed. It was a running gag between the two of us and his way of telling me I had better take care of my teeth or it was going to happen to me too.

We ate quietly for a few moments, and I tried to think of a way to say what I had come to talk to him about.

"Do you think Constance is one of those alcoholics?"

"What?" he asked.

"You know . . . where they have to go to a sanitarium and get dried out and all that stuff?"

"Oh, I don't think she's that bad off," he said. "Looks like she just goes on a binge once in a while and can't handle it."

"Boy, she sure did yesterday." I had already told him what had happened.

"I guess she takes after her old man," he said. "He used to blow his top when he was hittin' the bottle. One time when Constance was about your age, her mother had a lot of ladies out from Omaha for tea, and Constance was playing the piano for 'em, and old Jesse came downstairs all boozed up. He walked right into the living room in nothing but his B.V.D.'s and told 'em all to shut up because he was trying to take a nap. Then he took his gun—he had this five-hundred dollar hunting rifle, all gold inlaid and carved—and he shot up every teacup in the room. They said the old biddies screamed like mad and ducked behind the sofas and thought they were all going to get killed. Nobody got hurt, but I guess they were picking bullets out of the woodwork for months."

I didn't say anything for a moment. At first the story had seemed funny, but then I wondered what I would have done if it had been me in that living room playing the piano.

"I wonder what Constance did," I said.

"I bet she quit playing the piano real quick," Dad laughed.

It didn't strike me funny. "I bet she cried," I said quietly.

Dad looked over at me thoughtfully. "I suppose so," he said. "She must have had a hard time of it."

"I feel kinda sorry for her," I said. I waited a second, then plunged into it. "Listen, Dad. Wouldn't it be great if we could invite her to stay at our house for a few days until she feels better?"

"Don't start that," he said, giving me a sharp look. He realized that's what I had been leading up to.

"But, Dad . . . it would cheer her up to be around other people."

"Forget it!"

"She could have your room, and you could sleep on the sofa."

"What?" he said incredulously.

"Just for a few days?"

"No!"

"Let's ask her, please?"

"We can't have her at our house!" he said. "What would people think?"

"Who cares what other people think?" I said. "Couldn't we?"

"No!" he said again.

"Just for a few days?" I repeated.

"Now don't harp at me," he said angrily.

"Well, I think we should do something to help her," I said stubbornly. Now that Grandma's ideas had taken hold, I wasn't about to give them up so quickly.

He got up and started to climb back into the crane.

"Get out of here," he said irritably. "I gotta get back to work!"

"Dad," I said, climbing up after him. "Could I at least go over and she if she's OK?"

"No!"

"She looks like she might be sick."

"I don't want you going over there."

"We could stop by after you finish work, OK?"

"We?" he said.

"I'll just look in to see if she's all right."

"No!" he said firmly.

"Please, Dad?"

"I'm not going over there and neither are you!" he said angrily. "I don't want you to have anything more to do with her."

I climbed right onto the seat next to him, and he gave me one of his exasperated looks. He knew I wasn't going to give up so easily.

We drove up to the Gunderson house in Dad's old red pickup shortly after five.

"Just see if she's OK," Dad said. "I don't want you going in and staying . . ."

"OK," I answered, and got out of the truck and went up and knocked on the door. I waited a few moments, looked back at Dad and shrugged. I knocked again.

Finally the door opened, and there stood Constance, looking pale and disheveled. She was barefoot and wearing a faded old bathrobe. When she saw me, she left the door standing open and turned away and moved back into the hallway as though she didn't want me to see her.

"Hi," I said. "I just wondered if you needed anything."

She kept her face turned away from me. "I'm so sorry about what happened yesterday, Addie."

"That's OK."

"No, it isn't," she said. "It was a terrible thing to do to you." She walked slowly over to the big staircase and stood at the foot of the steps as though she were going up to the second floor. "I hope you know I didn't mean all those awful things I said."

"I was pretty sure you didn't," I said. "I didn't mean what I said either."

"I was feeling low," she said. "I lost a job and I just took it out on the next person I saw, and that was you."

Just then, Dad came in the door behind me to see what was keeping me, and she looked up and saw him. She seemed humiliated. She looked at me again and spoke to both of us.

"I'm not a Broadway star. I can't even get a job as an actress. I work as a hostess in a restaurant . . . and not even a very good restaurant."

I was so shocked I couldn't say a word. I knew it must have been terribly painful for her to admit her failure, especially in front of Dad, and I admired her courage. Suddenly she put her hand to her forehead as though she felt faint and quickly sat down on the steps.

"You OK?" I asked.

"Yes," she said. "Just a little dizzy. I haven't felt like eating for the past couple of days."

I looked at Dad and he looked down at me with a troubled

expression. I knew he realized now that she really was ill, and he knew we couldn't just walk away and leave her there alone. He didn't like being stuck with this problem, but he had to do something.

I looked at him again. I knew it would be easy enough for me to say something, but I wanted him to do it, and I waited him out. There was an awkward silence—Constance sitting forlornly on the step, her head down, Dad watching her, and me watching him. Finally, he couldn't stand the silence any more, and he spoke.

"I think you'd better come home with us and stay a few days."

I almost cheered out loud. I couldn't believe he had broken down and done it.

"Oh, I couldn't," Constance said to him.

"You can't stay here all alone like this," he said, and walked over to her at the foot of the stairs. "I mean, we'd be glad to have you." Then he reached out his hand as though to help her up.

She looked up at him, and I think she understood how difficult it had been for him to offer his help.

"Thank you, James," she said quietly, and she took his hand.

It was odd, but in that moment, I somehow felt that Constance had helped Dad as much as he had helped her.

Dad moved his things into the living room and Constance stayed in his room for three days. I took her meals to her on a tray. On the third day, when she felt up to it, she sat up in bed with pillows at her back, and I sat at the foot of the bed and sketched her. I wouldn't let her see the sketch until it was all finished.

"I don't think I want to see it anyway," she said. "I must look like something the cat dragged in."

"No, you don't!" I said. "You look lots better today."

She did look better too. The few days of rest had done wonders for her, and her beautiful face seemed softer and more relaxed. She was wearing Grandma's best pink flannel nightgown, and her hair was brushed softly back from her face.

She smiled. "A few days of your grandma's cooking would make anybody feel better." She looked over at the daffodils I had put on her breakfast tray.

"You know, the other day when you brought me those daffodils," she said, "it brought back so many memories. I remember being in New York one spring, and broke. I had just been to an audition, and I knew I had been terrible. There was a man on the street selling flowers. And I thought, if I could just have some daffodils, that would be some small bit of beauty in my life. But I didn't have the fifty cents to buy them." She paused and looked at me. "But if I had just come home, I wouldn't have had to long for things like that. They were right here for the taking."

"Why didn't you come home?" I asked, putting down my sketch pad to listen.

"I was ashamed," she said. "I didn't want anyone to know the truth. I never had a lead on Broadway. I never got anything but small parts in Shakespeare, and that didn't pay very much. The only time I was a leading lady was in a crummy stock company." She smiled sadly at the memory. "Mom and Dad wanted me to come home and get married and settle down, but I stayed on and kept trying. I was too stubborn and proud to ask them for help. When they finally realized I wasn't going to give up, they started making up stories about how successful I was."

"How come?" I asked.

"They just couldn't accept the fact that I was a failure. And I kept hoping for that big break, but it just never happened. I remember one winter . . . I lived in an unfurnished apartment with no heat or hot water. I slept in a sleeping bag on the floor, and cooked in the ice-cube tray."

I laughed at the idea, and she smiled at me.

"I guess it sounds like fun to you," she said. "I think some of it was, for a while. But the cold . . . you have no idea how cold it was. And the worst part was being afraid somebody might find out I was a failure."

She wasn't smiling now, and I knew it must be very difficult for her to tell me about it. "Didn't you miss your mom and dad?" I asked.

"Yes, I did. When my mother died a few weeks ago, I just felt . . ." She let the sentence trail off, as though it were too painful to finish. "We never had time to know each other," she said.

"But why didn't you do something else, if you didn't like the jobs you got?" I asked.

"Oh, Addie," she said sadly, "it's so easy to lose sight of your goal. She looked at me for a moment, and I had the feeling that she almost didn't want to trouble me with what she was about to say.

"You go off to be an artist," she went on, "and it's such a long, hard climb that you can get caught up in the struggle itself, and then just surviving becomes the goal. It's hard to think much about truth and beauty when you don't have enough food on the table. That's when your dreams slip through your fingers."

She stopped for a moment, and I said nothing. I knew what she was saying was very painful for her.

"When I came home," she said, "I guess it all hit me at once . . . all my family gone and twenty years with nothing to show for it. That's what set off the drinking spree, I suppose. I just felt like everything was finished for me. I felt I was nothing."

She began to cry, and for a moment I didn't move, not knowing how to help her. I reached for a handkerchief from the night table and gave it to her.

"I don't think you're nothing," I said, and I sat on the bed beside her. "I think you're one of the most terrific people I ever met. The other day . . . when you acted for us . . . I never saw anyone do anything like that before. It gave me chills. I thought . . . if I could ever make anybody feel like that with one of my paintings . . . then I'd really be an artist."

She looked up at me.

"I think you're beautiful," I said, and hugged her, and she put her arms around me and held me close.

Chapter Seven

THE NEXT DAY WAS SATURDAY, the day before Easter, and Dad and Grandma and I were sitting around the kitchen table finishing our breakfast. We hadn't heard Constance stirring around and guessed she was still asleep. I was putting some last little touches on my drawing of her as I sat at the table.

"What are you wearing to church tomorrow, Grandma?" I asked.

"My good blue dress . . . like last Easter," she replied. Grandma seldom got dressed up, so a "good" dress lasted her for years.

"Oh, yeah," I said. "I like that one. We'll both be blue. Dad, what are you wearing?"

"I'll be blue too," he said. "I've only got one good summer suit, and that's blue." He looked ominously toward his bedroom. "If I can get into my room to get it."

"Oh, Dad!" I said. "She's only been here a few days!"

He had been grumping around about Constance displacing him to the sofa, but I reminded him that he was the one who invited her, and Grandma kept telling him what a nice thing it had been for him to do. He seemed a little embarrassed by the fact that he had been so soft-hearted, but I think he was actually rather pleased with himself. Of course, he would never let anyone else know that. Grandma and I didn't really take his complaining about Constance too seriously; it was just his nature to look on the dark side of everything. I think he figured that in case things didn't work out, he would always be able to say that he had been the first one to suspect something was wrong.

I put the last stroke to my drawing, looked at it for a moment, and then held it out to Grandma. "How's this?" I asked.

She came closer and adjusted her glasses to get a good look at it. "Oh, my, isn't that good! Looks just like her."

I held it out to Dad. "Yeah, not bad," he said. For him, that was lavish praise.

"Can I see it too?"

We all turned, and there was Constance standing in the doorway. It was the first time she had been up and around since she had come to stay with us. She was wearing a soft green silk blouse and green slacks and looked lovely.

"You're up!" I said, running over to her and showing her the drawing.

She looked at it for a moment and then at me. "You're really very good, Addie," she said.

She sat down at the table, and I got her some coffee.

"You don't want to overdo, now," Grandma said to her. "You'll have to take it easy."

"I don't know how to thank all of you for everything you've done," Constance said.

"It's little enough to do for a friend of the family," Grandma said.

"I'm going to have to think about getting back to New York," Constance said.

"I wish you wouldn't go!" I said. "Why don't you stay in Clear River for a while?"

"Why would she want to stay here?" Dad asked, as though it were ridiculous.

"She likes it here!" I said impatiently.

"Well, at least I know New York, and I know people there," said Constance. "It's where my life is, I guess."

"Now, Constance," said Grandma. "You know lots of people right here in Clear River too, and you have a house here, after all. I think Addie's right . . . you ought to think of stayin' on. You'd have some peace and quiet here and get rested up."

"Oh, I wish you'd stay here and teach dramatics!" I said. "We could use somebody artistic around here."

"You and your wild ideas," Dad said.

I made a face at him.

"I think it's a nice idea," said Grandma. "Young folks would be glad to have help from someone like Constance."

Constance smiled. "I think it's a little late in life for me to start something like that."

"Grandma says you're never too old to change," I said. "She started a new life when she was in her sixties. It's lucky for me she didn't think it was too late, or there's no telling where I'd be now. I think you should stay."

"It's a lovely daydream, Addie," Constance said, shaking her head.

"Well, at least you'll be here tomorrow, won't you?" I asked. "And you can come to Easter church services with us?"

"I don't think so," she said.

"Please!"

"I've got nothing to wear," she said, trying to put me off.

"What's the matter with that dress you wore over here to supper the other night?" Dad asked suddenly. He had just blurted it out and then looked embarrassed. I couldn't believe he had said it! I had never heard him compliment any woman on how she looked. Grandma shot him a funny look over the top of her glasses.

Dad tried to cover his embarrassment. "I mean . . . it looked pretty good to me . . ." he trailed off, not knowing how to get out of it.

Constance went to his rescue and gave him a lovely smile.

"Thank you, James," she said. "That's very nice of you to say so, but I doubt if I could show my face in this town now."

"You shouldn't give a fig what folks think, Constance!" Grandma said. "You did the best you could, and if it didn't all work out, so what? You tried, that's all that's important. Besides, this is your home."

Constance looked at Grandma thoughtfully and smiled.

The next morning, Dad was up early and nagging us to get ready for church on time. Constance had finally agreed to go with us, and I had a feeling Dad wanted to get there early so we wouldn't have to make an entrance in front of everybody with Constance.

As a result, the four of us were almost the first ones there, and we sat in the hard pews of the First Baptist Church of Clear River for almost fifteen minutes waiting for services to begin. Finally, the church filled up around us, and I felt everyone looking over at us, astounded to see Constance at all, let alone with the three of us.

Carla Mae's family sat at the other end of our pew, and Carla Mae and I managed to slide over next to each other so we could harmonize on the hymns. She sang second soprano and I sang alto. As soon as we got into high school, we were going to join the church choir, and we wanted to be as well prepared as possible.

There had been no chance to introduce Constance to anyone before the service, and as we all left the church and everyone stood around talking on the sidewalk outside, I planned to have her meet the other people. But everyone just nodded and walked on by us, and I suddenly realized that they had no intention of making her feel welcome.

I tried to pretend that nothing had happened, but I could tell Constance was aware of what was going on. It must have been very painful for her, but she was too good an actress to show that her feelings were hurt. The four of us stood there alone, like a little island in the midst of all the other people passing by. I wanted to grab her hand and run away, and I could tell Dad was feeling uncomfortable too.

Just then, Mrs. Coyne was coming our way. I thought she would pass us by too, especially after what had happened at the style show. But she came right up to us and said hello to Constance as though nothing had ever happened.

I remembered what she had said about Constance being an old friend, and I thought they must have liked each other a lot for the friendship to have lasted all those years. I knew everyone

was watching because Mrs. Coyne was one of the most influential ladies in the church. After she had said hello to Constance, she turned and called over several other people. At first they were hesitant, but Mrs. Coyne was insistent, and finally they approached and she introduced them to Constance. Once the ice was broken, curiosity got the best of people, and more of them came over to say hello. Then the preacher, Reverend Barrett, came out, and Mrs. Coyne introduced him to Constance, too.

Constance was suddenly besieged with people wanting to meet her. Dad and Grandma and I looked at each other with hopeful smiles on our faces. I wasn't sure what everyone really thought of Constance or what they would say behind her back later, but she was gracious to them all, and I knew it was at least a beginning.

Tanya, Carla Mae and Gloria gathered around, and I held my chin up high and stood proudly beside Constance in my blue rickrack dress.

Epilogue

CONSTANCE NEVER DID GO BACK to New York; she decided to stay on in Clear River. Grandma had been right about everybody having a chance to start a new life.

But it wasn't easy for Constance. She never did exactly fit in. Of course, that's what made her a special person . . . Constance did what was right for her, and she didn't care what anybody thought. Once the town calmed down about her being there, she began teaching drama and piano to the children. Going to her classes became one of the high points of our lives.

Constance enriched those years for us, and somehow I think we enriched her life too.

I finally did go to New York to work as an artist, and when things were difficult, I would remember what Constance had said about not letting your dreams slip through your fingers. I held on to my dreams, and I was never afraid to go back to Clear River.